THE CIRCUS THIEF

Written by **Alane Adams**

Illustrated by **Lauren Gallegos**

SparkPress
80 E. Rio Salado Pkwy, Suite 511
Tempe, AZ 85281
www.gosparkpress.com

Printed in the United States of America

Library of Congress Cataloging-in-Publication Data
Adams, Alane.
The Circus Thief / Alane Adams; Illustrated by Lauren Gallegos. — 1st ed.
p. cm.
ISBN 978-1-943006-75-5

First Edition
Book design by Lauren Gallegos

For Baby Cash —A.A.

For Renee —L.G.

Summer, 1929
Girard, Pennsylvania

Georgie peeked into the kitchen. Papa sat at the table eating his supper. Mama was washing dishes at the sink.

He stepped into the room. "Papa, can I talk to you?"

"What is it, son?"

"It's just . . ." Georgie crept closer. "I've done all my chores this week. I picked up the eggs and fed the pigs."

Papa frowned. "And I suppose you think you deserve a reward for that?"

Georgie nodded. "I think it would be nice if you gave me a dollar."

There was silence. Mama stopped washing dishes. Papa set his fork down.

"Now why would I give you a dollar for something you ought to do? Should I charge you for that new pair of shoes you're wearing?"

Georgie looked down at his shiny boots. "No, Papa."

"Should I charge you for that new coat I bought you?"

"No." Georgie shuffled his feet. "It's just, the circus is in town and I was hoping I could go."

Papa's eyebrows went up. "The circus is in town, you say?"

Georgie stepped closer. "Yes, sir. There's going to be a man that gets shot out of a cannon." Georgie had read all about it on a poster at the hardware store. There were even going to be elephants!

Papa rubbed his jaw. "And you say you did all your chores this week?"

"Yes, sir. Just ask Mama." Georgie held his breath as he looked at Mama.

Mama nodded as she wiped a dish. "It's true, Papa. Why he fairly flew out the door this morning to feed those chickens."

Papa picked up his fork and went back to his supper. "Maybe we can check it out. See what all the fuss is about. I always did love the circus."

The next day, Georgie could barely wait for breakfast to be over. His friend Harley waited outside for him.

"Did he really say you could go?" Harley said, hopping from foot to foot.

"Yup." Georgie had hardly slept a wink the night before.

"Boy, I wish I could go. I hear there's a lady with a beard. Can you imagine that?"

Papa came out holding his keys. He nodded at Harley. "What are you doing here, boy?"

Georgie jumped up. "Papa, can Harley go with us? Please?"

Harley kicked at the dirt. "It's okay. I don't have any money for a ticket."

Papa just sighed. "Get in the truck. Both of you."

Georgie grinned at Harley, and the two boys hurried to the truck before Papa changed his mind.

The circus had set up their tents on the edge of town. Flags fluttered and flapped in the breeze. An elephant walked by on large grey legs and let out a loud trumpet blast with its trunk.

Harley's eyes grew round. "Did you see that, Georgie? It was an elephant! A real live elephant."

It was the biggest animal Georgie had ever seen.

Papa bought their tickets and then
waved to some men he knew.

"You boys behave. I'll see you back
here after the show."

Harley dragged Georgie forward.
"Come on, let's get a good seat."

They made their way inside the tent and wiggled their way onto a bench up front.

The place grew quiet as the ringmaster came out.

"Ladies and gentlemen, I present to you the most Royal of Arabian Steeds, L-a-a-a-dy Roxie."

The curtains parted and a beautiful white horse with purple silk tassels came prancing out. She made a full circle around the ring, and then came to a stop in front of the two boys.

"Roxie, take a bow," the ringmaster said.

Roxie bent her front leg back and bowed her head low, as if the boys were royalty.

"Did you see that?" Georgie said. "She was looking right at me."

"Nah, she was looking at me," Harley bragged.

The ringmaster continued. "Tonight will be the very last time Lady Roxie performs before she retires to green pastures and a lifetime supply of oats."

Roxie reared up and flashed her hooves in the air.

The ringmaster turned to her. "Tell us, Roxie, how old are you?"

The horse pawed the ground once, twice, three times, then waited.

The ringmaster made a face. "I think you're fibbing, Roxie. You're not three. Unless . . . " he held up a finger. "You were counting by fives."

Roxie tossed her head.

"Let's see, that's three times five, that makes . . ."

He hesitated and the crowd shouted, "Fifteen!"

"Fifteen, Roxie. Anymore?"

Roxie scratched her hoof two more times.

"Fifteen and two more . . . hmm . . . that makes—"

Georgie shot out of his seat. "Seventeen," he shouted.

The ringmaster turned and pointed at him. "That's right, young man. Step on down and join me."

Georgie grinned at Harley and then hopped over the rail. He walked up to Roxie and rubbed her nose. She whickered softly at him.

"Would you like to ride her?" the ringmaster asked. Georgie's eyes grew wide. "Would I? You bet."

He lifted Georgie onto her back. The horse trotted around the ring a few times as the crowd cheered.

Georgie waved as a crewman led her out of the ring. The curtain fell shut behind them. The crewman handed the reins off to a man in a black suit.

"It's the end of the line for you, Roxie," the man sneered. "You're too old to perform and the circus can't afford to feed you."

Georgie's heart dropped. "What do you mean?"

"This horse is going to the work farm."

"You can't do that." Georgie pulled back on the reins. "She's a trained circus horse."

The man tried to grab the reins, but Roxie reared up and took off like a rocket. Georgie held on for dear life. "Thief!" the man cried out. "That boy stole my horse." Roxie bolted across the field. Georgie tried to pull on the reins, but she wouldn't stop.

Then Papa was there, waving his hands in front of the horse. He grabbed the reins and slowed Roxie to a stop.

"Papa!" Georgie slipped down into his arms.

The man in the black suit ran up. There was a crowd with him. "That boy stole my horse."

"No, I didn't," Georgie said. "You scared her and she ran." Georgie looked up at Papa. "Please, Papa he's going to make her work till she drops. Do something."

Papa eyed Roxie from head to toe. "It seems a shame to waste such a beautiful animal." He ran his hand over Roxie's mane. "Perhaps we can come to an arrangement."

"Now see here, I paid for her fair and square," the man said.

"I reckon I can match what you paid." Papa opened his billfold and pulled out some bills, then added a few more. He crushed them into the other man's hand.

The man looked at the bills, then shook his fist at Papa and turned and left.

Harley burst through the crowd.
"What'd I miss?"
Georgie threw his arms around Roxie.
"We just bought ourselves a circus horse."